BRAZILIAN TEARS

and other poems

by

Fred W. Herman

*Our mission is to efficiently provide the world's finest, most comprehensive book publishing
service, enabling every author to experience success. To find out how to publish your
book, your way, and have it available worldwide, visit us online at www.trafford.com*

Trafford rev. 12/2/2009

 www.trafford.com

North America & international
toll-free: 1 888 232 4444 (USA & Canada)
phone: 250 383 6864 ♦ fax: 812 355 4082

Biography:

Fred Herman holds B.A. and M.A. degrees in English, has lived and studied in Europe and South America, and has taught modern languages in various colleges in an adjunct capacity.

Now retired, he lives in Worthington, Ohio, with his wife, Alice, and a rather independent-minded cat.

To my wife, Alice, whose endless patience and support made this work possible.

A note of appreciation should also be given to my teachers and tutors in England, whose help and advice enabled me to polish and fine-tune my creative work.

"It is the function of poetry to harmonize the sorrows of the world."

A.E. Housman

Contents

I	Brazilian Tears	1
II	Final Peace	2
III	Journey's End	3
IV	Never Again	4
V	One Last Red Rose	5
VI	The Acolyte's Only Friend	6
VII	The Little Girl's Farewell	7
VIII	The Oath	8
IX	The Present	9
X	Waiting For Father	10
XI	Word to the Wise	11
XII	The Oxford Lad and the London Lass	12
XIII	The Secret	13
XIV	Memories	14
XV	The Homecoming	15
XVI	Freedom's Shore	16

XVII	A Cup of Tea	17
XVIII	The Hero	18
XIX	Losing a Friend	19
XX	Losing the Mate	20
XXI	The Last Supper	21
XXII	Taking Kate for Mate	23
XXIII	Lies Inscribed in Stone	24
XXIV	Remembering the Blitz	25
XXV	Faith-based Madness	26
XXVI	Farewell	27
XXVII	The Prophet	28
XXVIII	Fortune's Final Quarter	29
XXIX	The Last Journey	30
XXX	Two Loving Sisters	31
XXXI	The Old Fisherman	32
XXXII	Labor's Reward	33
XXXIII	A Mother Kills Her Son	34
XXXIV	November Night	35
XXXV	The Cowboy	36

XXXVI	The Road to Nowhere	37
XXXVII	Sailor's Luck	38
XXXVIII	The Churchyard	39
XXXIX	More Supplies	40
XL	Return of the Sailor	41
XLI	Home-thoughts from the Sea	42
XLII	The Three Wretches	43
XLIII	Poor Edmund's Mother	44
XLIV	The Road Ahead	45
XLV	A Child's Dream	46
XLVI	The Epitaph	47
XLVII	The Shadow That Couldn't Hear	48
XLVIII	The Cleansing	49
XLIX	Old Man At Christmas	50

I
Brazilian Tears

As a child her mother had taught her to pray,
But then her mother had died.
And she remembers how she had cried,
For she had nothing left with which to pay
For the priest to come
To say Mass for the dead.
When she had a child, it was all that she had,
For the man she had loved had long since gone,
And it seemed that everyone
Had denied her a roof and a piece of bread,
And the priest would only come
To say Mass for the dead.
But now her child is also dead,
For she lived in a forbidding slum
Where no one would ever come
To help with a piece of bread,
And even the priest would no longer come
To say Mass for the dead.
So she dreams of all that she might have had,
But she has no money for a piece of bread,
And she prays that she will soon be dead
So the priest can come
To say Mass for the dead.

II
Final Peace

Homeward bound, the sailor on deck
Had nothing left to do but count
The endless days to take him back
To family and long-neglected friends.

While still in port, he thought to check
The bloodstained picture that he found
While scrounging through an empty shack
Abandoned by the water's edge:

A stranger's face, battle-worn and strained,
Tormented and prepared for death's domain,
Where only blood and gore remained,
And no one ever cared . . .

It was an image of the other side.
And so he flung it swiftly and without a sound
Into the jaws of the forgiving tide,
To grant the stranger final peace.

III
Journey's End

I think the man is dying.
Can't you see his failing breath,
His legs just barely trying
To complete the race with death?

Give him the cup to taste,
Perhaps it will refresh him
Just enough to fly in haste
Before old Nick can gain on him.

He's kneeling at the rail at length,
To put his soul at ease
And taste the cup for strength
To go where he will find his peace.

IV
Never Again

When people tend to bend with the wind,
They will often let go to be scattered
Like dry autumn leaves or a sly band
Of thieves to some far away spot
Where an unkind fate will just leave them to rot.

But how can a boy forget the furious
Winds of the war, or the soldiers
With their endless shouting, their officious spouting,
And their boots stomping on the floor
Until, like the wind, they were gone once more.

And what good are the weighty words of the wise
If they're just as fleeting as the wind,
When the boy, later that dreary night,
To add to his plight, found his mother
With the lifeless body of his only brother.

Yet the boy will never forget the fear
And the oppressive darkness outside,
And the all-pervading stench of death
When he held this breath as he fled in turn,
Convinced that he would never return.

V
One Last Red Rose

When first I spied the red-haired girl
I wanted her to be my bride.
So I gave her one red rose to hold,
As I held her by my side.

And when I wed the red-haired girl
I gave her one red rose to hold
In her fragile little hand,
And she was lovely to behold.

If fate should wrest my red-haired girl
From my withered, shaking hand,
I'll get her one more rose to hold,
For death will triumph in the end.

VI
The Acolyte's Only Friend

Hidden from sight in an empty stable stall
A heavy hutch was stashed against a wall.
And in it crouched a furry creature of the night,
Smuggled there in secret by the acolyte,
Who loved the vicious sharp-fanged beast,
Which was not sanctioned by the local priest.

Hidden from sight and the light of silent stars,
The beast was watching through the iron bars
The shameful scars inflicted on the hapless acolyte
As deadly silence ruled the dreadful night,
And youthful trust betrayed by a wicked priest,
Who never liked the fearsome sharp-fanged beast.

But youthful trust was finally rewarded
When the hidden hutch was left unguarded,
And the watchful beast espied the unlocked gate
Which quickly sealed the lustful cleric's fate.
But the trusting youth just watched the stunning feast,
For his only friend was the fearsome sharp-fanged beast.

VII
The Little Girl's Farewell

Please keep my doll and let her stay;
I know that you will treat her well.
She always smiled when I was sad,
But now I have to go away.

Please let her stay with you a spell,
For I shall have to go away.
And hold her little hand for me;
I fear I cannot say farewell.

So keep my little doll for me
Until I shall return for her,
When you can place my little doll
Into the box where I shall be.

VIII
The Oath

They came to celebrate that July night
Where everybody yelled and laughed,
And the darkened sky turned red and bright
With flames and fireworks galore,
Only his small house was there no more.

And all he could remember of that July night
Where everybody yelled and laughed,
How his small child had screamed for him and cried,
And so he swore he would return once more
Someday, with fireworks galore.

And so he rushed to town that next July,
Where everybody yelled and laughed,
And all the pines that night stood tall and dry,
But in the flames he heard his child once more,
And then the town was there no more.

IX
The Present

High on a hill and hidden from view,
They lived in a shack, seen by so few.
So I gave some coins to the mother
And a toy to the girl's little brother,
Who took it gladly, and then he smiled.

But the girl in the back of the shack
Just leaned on her crutch and didn't smile back.
For the life she had lived, she couldn't forgive,
And I feared I had nothing more left to give
To the girl who had never smiled.

But then I remembered the little chain
With the tiny cross, to help ease the pain.
And it seemed that the gift had the Virgin's touch,
As the girl came forward without her crutch,
And all of a sudden, she smiled.

X
Waiting For Father

To be on hand when his father arrived,
The boy had always contrived
To be there on the very day
When the ship was due to dock
At about two o'clock . . .
Unless there was some delay.

He did not want to be deprived
Of being first when the ship arrived;
For it always was such a glorious day.
He was sure, that the ship would dock
No later than two o'clock . . .
And why should there be a delay?

Later that day, when the news arrived
That none had survived
The storm of the previous day,
The boy at the end of the dock
Was still there . . . way past two o'clock . . .
Convinced, it was just a delay.

XI
Word to the Wise

Why are you so sad my friend,
When death is all you ever sought
For those who do not share your thought
On what you think the powerful commend?

You taught your sons that final worth
Is found in slaying those who do not share
What you believe the powerful declare
To be ordained on earth.

Your sons did follow your advice to slay
All those who never shared your view
And deal them what you think should be their due
If they should dare to seek another way.

So grieve no more, beloved friend,
For now your precious sons are dead.
No longer can they go and shed
The blood of those who seek a better end.

XII
The Oxford Lad and the London Lass

She thought her Oxford lad was smart
Because he tried so very hard
To give her what she most desired.
But Oxford didn't teach him
What's required
To satisfy a London lass
Who yearned for more
Than just a piece of . . .
Well, whatever;
Oxford men just aren't that clever.

XIII
The Secret

I still remember all those years
Of endless wars, of fears, of untold dead,
But our mother never said
That she once had another son.

And had he been allowed to live,
He would have been my older brother,
A savage fighter, like none other,
But mother fought another war.

And so, before she closed her eyes
That final time, her voice
Grew faint: "I didn't have a choice,"
She said, "There were too many dead."

And yet, how will we ever know
How many people are alive today
Because he never saw the light of day?
There were no tears …. And then she died.

XIV
Memories

"Do not forsake me, o my darling,"
Was the tune she used to hum.
But I couldn't spare a farthing
When I was innocent and young.

"Do not forsake me," was the tune
She used to hum, as we walked
Through the silent hills that noon,
And paused, held hands, and talked.

Oh, how I miss those sky-blue eyes,
Those lips so soft and red,
As we said our final goodbyes.
And that I'll remember until I am dead.

XV
The Homecoming

Home from the wars,
After endless years
Of faithfully following the flag,
He had already shed his tears
For friends who had returned before
In a cost-effective plastic bag.

No family was there to greet him
On the dock when he returned.
Just some strangers spouting boring speeches
To the weary wanderer, who only yearned
To join the many friends he'd lost
On bloody foreign beaches.

XVI
Freedom's Shore

Come on my boy,
Make haste, don't cry,
Let us to freedom fly.
There is no other way.

The boat is small,
So come what may,
Trust in the sea and pray.
There is no other way.

So they set out to sea,
No slaves were they to be.
But close to freedom's shore
Their boat was there no more,
For fate had ruled the day.

XVII
A Cup of Tea

You must not read this sinful book,
My faith does not allow for it.
Even so you say you can't just quit
This wicked college course you took.

Just brew a cup of tea instead
And make it very strong,
To make me feel that you belong.
So make the tea and go to bed.

The tea was strong as strong can be,
But no one knew about the bane,
For not all teas are quite the same:
It was a bitter cup of tea.

The witch was just too hard to please.
And so he fixed the tea all by himself,
But left no remnant on the shelf . . .
Then watched her drink – and sleep in peace.

XVIII
The Hero

Both my legs are gone.
They shot them off . . .
Not all at once,
But one by bloody one.

There's not much left
Of me, so if you wish
For me to stay away
And let me rot bereft

I shall not fault you,
Whatever you decide.
But I shall never
Stop to think of you . . .

. . . I am aware you are not whole,
But I shall wed you
Just the same, as long as
You have kept your truthful soul.

XIX
Losing a Friend

I shall not be here for long,
My days are numbered:
It's time to say good-bye.

Your friendly smile will do,
For I am going home,
So do not cry.

You must have faith,
For I shall go where I belong.
It's time to say good-bye.

A simple marker shall suffice,
With just my name,
And not much else.

XX
Losing the Mate

Their sturdy ship was lost . . .
And they prayed that they'd be spared
By the unforgiving sea.
But no one really cared
Where their hated mate could be.

Although the crew was safe,
There was still some space
For him in the heaving boat.
But there was no trace
Of him in the raging sea.

When they left their sinking ship
The mate was still on his bunk.
And they were pretty sure
That he was ungodly drunk
When he dived into the raging sea.

He was swimming as fast as he could,
Though it was clear to everyone
That he was as drunk as drunk can be.
But then their hated mate was gone.
Swallowed by the merciless sea.

XXI
The Last Supper

Down the aisle
With nose up high
Smelling the air,
Running here and there,
One hungry mouse
Was peeking through the rail.

There was a sound . . .
Was someone there
To snatch whatever consecrated morsel
May have dropped by chance
From yonder blessed table?

But it was too late . . .
For sustenance is not confined
To pious mice alone,
No matter how deserving.
But other critters, big in size,
With room to spare for more
Than just one measly mouse.

So all that's left
Of one small virtuous mouse
Were two small legs
Attached to one behind
With just a tail attached
For us to find.

XXII
Taking Kate for Mate

As soon as they were introduced
He took his giggling Kate in tow.
But little did he really know
That she had him at once reduced

To where all help would come too late.
As neighbors cheered, and bets were cast
On how the whole affair would last
When he took luscious Kate for mate.

So when at last he went to jump
Right into bed with luscious Kate,
His gorgeous and seductive mate,
He was of course ungodly drunk.

And so he missed, and banged his head
On the unforgiving floor instead.

XXIII
Lies Inscribed in Stone

If all those long forgotten buried bodies
Were resurrected and allowed to join
The living now, we all may have to share the blame
With those who once bore our precious name.

But all those long forgotten rotten bullies
Lie buried next to their incorrigible mates
To cool them off and keep their peace once more
And hold their wicked tongues forevermore.

Since ancient feuds are better kept below
A canopy of patient soggy dirt,
We can ignore the lies inscribed in stone
Of those who never had an honest bone.

XXIV
Remembering the Blitz

We knew he was a continental clown
Who hoped to lick old London town.
But even though his shirt was brown
Charlie Chaplin was the better clown.

XXV
Faith-based Madness

And it was decreed
That war was good and not to be delayed,
And so they bowed their heads and prayed:

War is gracious, just look at the flags . . .
And war is ever so kind
To those who are left behind.
O thank you Lord for lovely war,
To make us richer evermore.

And so it will forever be
According to some high decree,
And so it will forever be.

XXVI
Farewell

Please have a cup of tea on me
Until we meet again,
For now my ship will have to sail.

So have a cup of tea on me
And hope that we shall meet again,
For true love will prevail.

XXVII
The Prophet

Way up in the steeple of an ancient church,
Next to the silent prayer bell,
A raven sits on his lofty perch
Cawing and squawking for fare-thee-well,
Inviting us mockingly to join him in hell.

When cunningly chanting a pious reply,
The vicar starts ringing the prayer bell,
But the raven insists that it's just a big lie.
And as far as anyone else can tell
It may all be a gimmick concocted in hell.

XXVIII
Fortune's Final Quarter

The dreamy girl at the end of the dock
Was carelessly churning the water,
But she paid no heed to the clock
As it ominously struck the quarter.

Attracted to the playful splashing
In the pure and silent water,
An enchanted swan came thrashing
When the clock struck the second quarter.

Impressed by the show of power
And beguiled by Fortune's daughter,
She didn't heed the fateful hour
When it struck another quarter.

And when she was lured off the dock
Without murmur and into the water,
Only the ominous sound of the clock
Announced Fortune's final quarter.

XXIX
The Last Journey

The boy had hoped to see the ship
Whose name had captured every heart.
For this would be her final trip,
Before they cut her all apart.

At last the gorgeous ship was due.
Her swelling sails appeared sublime.
The father watched the busy crew,
The boy slept soundly all the time.

The father's tiny tugboat slaved.
Misfortune made the ships collide.
The father and men were saved . . .
The boy was still asleep inside.

XXX
Two Loving Sisters

The girl tried hard to keep her man
Although it was a hopeless task.
Her clever sister spoiled her plan
And lured the man with smiling mask.

But when her sister died one night,
Detectives pounced upon the lad.
The girl went free, to her delight.
It cost her lover's neck instead.

XXXI
The Old Fisherman

They carried him home in a big red sail.
A bundle of clothing that he had worn
Was all that was left by the raging gale.

They carried him back where he once was born,
But no one was left, and the night was still,
And all they could do was to sit and mourn.

They carried him up in the morning's chill
And buried him deep in a hidden spot,
Forgotten and lost on a naked hill.

They left him behind in his grassy plot,
And that was the best in the old man's lot.

XXXII
Labor's Reward

All week
We catch some fish
For them to eat.
But then
They'd rather have
Some meat.

But woe,
Should we return
With empty hold.
What they
Would say, need not
Be told.

XXXIII
A Mother Kills Her Son

He used to be a gentle lad,
And everybody liked him well.
The story of his life was sad,
As every man in town could tell.

His brother was his mother's pride.
And he tried hard to be like him.
She always took his brother's side,
The feud she caused was deep and grim.

He always was a little frail,
So he sat out to prove to them
That he could triumph and not fail.
Their childish smiles he meant to stem.

In view of every boy in town
He swam until he lost his breath.
The murky river pulled him down,
But thus he died a hero's death.

XXXIV
November Night

An awful dream:
I could have sworn
That death was near.

I tried to scream.
But early dawn
Dispersed my fear.

XXXV
The Cowboy

A drifter came to town,
Who should have stayed away.
He saw the sheriff frown,
And drew without delay.

The drifter wanted more
Than just a lawman dead.
The bank seemed like a chore
He never had to dread.

He went and pulled his gun,
And did not smell the bait.
There lay behind a tun,
A crafty girl in wait.

She swiftly did her job,
And kissed him for a fee,
Then tossed him to the mob,
That hung him from a tree.

XXXVI
The Road to Nowhere

The road was rough and the speed was slow,
And his truck crept gently along the fence.
He lost his father a year ago,
And his mother a few days hence.

His little brother was sickly thence,
And he needed help for the lad.
He could not live just on providence,
So he took the job that his father had.

A load of dynamite was his bread.
Just a little while he had hoped to stay.
But the truck blew up and he too was dead,
And the lad soon followed him all the way.

XXXVII
Sailor's Luck

It happened just a year ago,
That I said farewell to Jenny Lee.
The western wind began to blow,
As the boat slid out to sea.

I dearly loved the bright-eyed lass,
But her mother did not care for me.
She said I was a common ass,
Who drifts about the sea.

And today I saw my love again,
With a bright-eyed lad upon her knee.
With all my hope and love in vain:
I have lost my Jenny Lee.

XXXVIII
The Churchyard

Within the churchyard, one by one,
Are many long low graves.
And stones are crowning every one,
On some the green grass waves.

So many Christian children lie
Relieved of earthly pain.
Whenever we shall pass them by,
We'll pray for them again.

They do not join in worldly fun,
They do not see us pass.
They cannot feel the warm bright sun,
That shines upon the grass.

When silence shrouds the grassy mound,
And naked earth their bed,
Then death has won the final round.
For us they will be dead.

XXXIX
More Supplies

Smothered by the southern sun
Rests a faithful heart.
He was just another one
Who had to depart.

Silently the fever came
To the mining camp,
As death staked out a claim.
And he was our champ.

Miners pay no heed to cries,
Ore does not know pain.
Ships unload still more supplies:
Immigrants from Spain.

XL
Return of the Sailor

The sea is black, the coast is grey,
And yonder lies the town.
The boat is entering the bay,
The fog seeps slowly down.

The bow creeps gently up the sound
I have not seen all year.
My eyes are scouting all around,
My sweetheart should be here.

I see the sheds, the quay, a crane.
To hold her just once more . . .
I look, I search, but all in vain.
I see no soul ashore.

I hear a buoy with empty clank.
My legs are made of lead.
I wearily walk down the plank.
My sweetheart must be dead.

XLI
Home-thoughts from the Sea

When I come home to you
From my trip across the sea,
What a lovely couple we shall be.
A world just for us two.

If those years of hope come true
It will be a thrill to see
You smile and wait for me.
When I come home to you.

XLII
The Three Wretches

Three wretches went to seek their luck
Deep in the forest's domain,
Where one looked for pleasure,
And one went for treasure,
With the third for baser gain.

The three went out to test their luck
And challenge the forest's domain.
But two caught the fever,
Which left the believer
In baser gain.

And he went on to try his luck
In the silent forest of rain,
Where he caught his prey
To be taken away
For baser gain.

But a furious arrow out of the rain
Sought out his quarry, which died in pain.

XLIII
Poor Edmund's Mother

You should not waste
Your time on books . . .
But Edmund liked to read
And did not heed
His mother's taste
For sports.

When Edmund grew to be a man
He left his mother's house
And found a girl with gorgeous looks,
Who also shared his love for books,
But did not care
For sports.

When Edmund's son was born
He did have gorgeous looks,
But did not care for books.
So Edmund, in despair,
Went home, to share
His mother's taste
For sports.

XLIV
The Road Ahead

For most of us it is the grave
To rest our worn-out bones.
But frequently we find some knave
Whose plot is marked with costly stones.

It may well be the end of life
Along a wicked road.
There are no cheers, no drums, no fife,
To line the pass he rode.

Yet life for some will just begin
And they are not alone.
For others, who have lived in sin,
There's no place near the throne.

We pass the graveyard one-by-one
And some go down to Hell.
For justice will be swiftly done
As every man can tell.

XLV
A Child's Dream

The night was dark, and the house was cold.
And in his room
The boy was alone with his tears,
Hoping that God
Would grant him a glimpse of the path
That his father had trod
In the distant world beyond the shadows
Of the valley of doom.

Then, out of the dark, and the damp,
And the dreary abode
Of the darkened skies, a gleam revealed the spot
Where his father was shot and left to rot
In a muddy ditch by a nameless road.

Ashen dawn dispersed the dream.
And on his cot
The trembling boy could feel the damp
Of the bloody spot.

XLVI
The Epitaph

Beneath this stone lie Johnny's bones
Whose heart was just a hard as all
The other stones.
A wicked man whose sun has set,
And not a single eye is wet.
No tears will moisten what remains.
He has to wait until it rains.

XLVII
The Shadow That Couldn't Hear

There was no need to use his ears.
He heard no shouts of friend or foe,
Because he had been deaf for years.

By night he left the town below
Along the path he knew by heart.
And late he reached the dark chateau.

A sentry played his cruel part.
He warned the shadow in the park,
Then shot the shepherd through the heart.

The sentry blamed it on the dark,
And cursed the night with some remark.

XLVIII
The Cleansing

When they came to rule the conquered land
They governed with an iron hand.
And there was endless talk about a dream,
And calls to join the new enlightened team
Of loyal soldiers to reform the vanquished world
And have a new, and unloved flag unfurled.

The land resounded with the endless lies
Of those in charge, to cover up the cries
Of untold victims all across the land,
Who were forever dealt a cruel hand.
But final victory will never come to those
Who force their will on non-believing foes.

The vanquished may lose all they once held dear
And though condemned to servitude and fear,
They soon will find a hidden ray of hope
To come their way and show them a new scope
To save them from their misery and endless pain,
And cleanse their land of bloody foreign stain.

XLIX
Old Man At Christmas

There was each year one special night
Of expectation, late in December.
The town was always calm and always bright.
Alone with his thoughts, the old man could remember
The joyous laughter and the great expectation… Long lost
Are the days of innocent childhood of so many years ago:
The happy memories of skating on rivers stiff with frost
And a world buried under a silent blanket of glistening snow.

The world was full of joy. The stars were bright,
And there were the endless swarms
Of noisy revelers . . . And the town below
Was drenched in festive noise and glittering light,
Where merry couples, on their way to warmth
And hearth, just passed him by, like drifting snow.